RISES THE MOON

A CRICKET-VERSE NOVELLA

WILLOW HADLEY

Edited by Taryn Gilliland

Cover Design by Maria Spada

❀ Created with Vellum

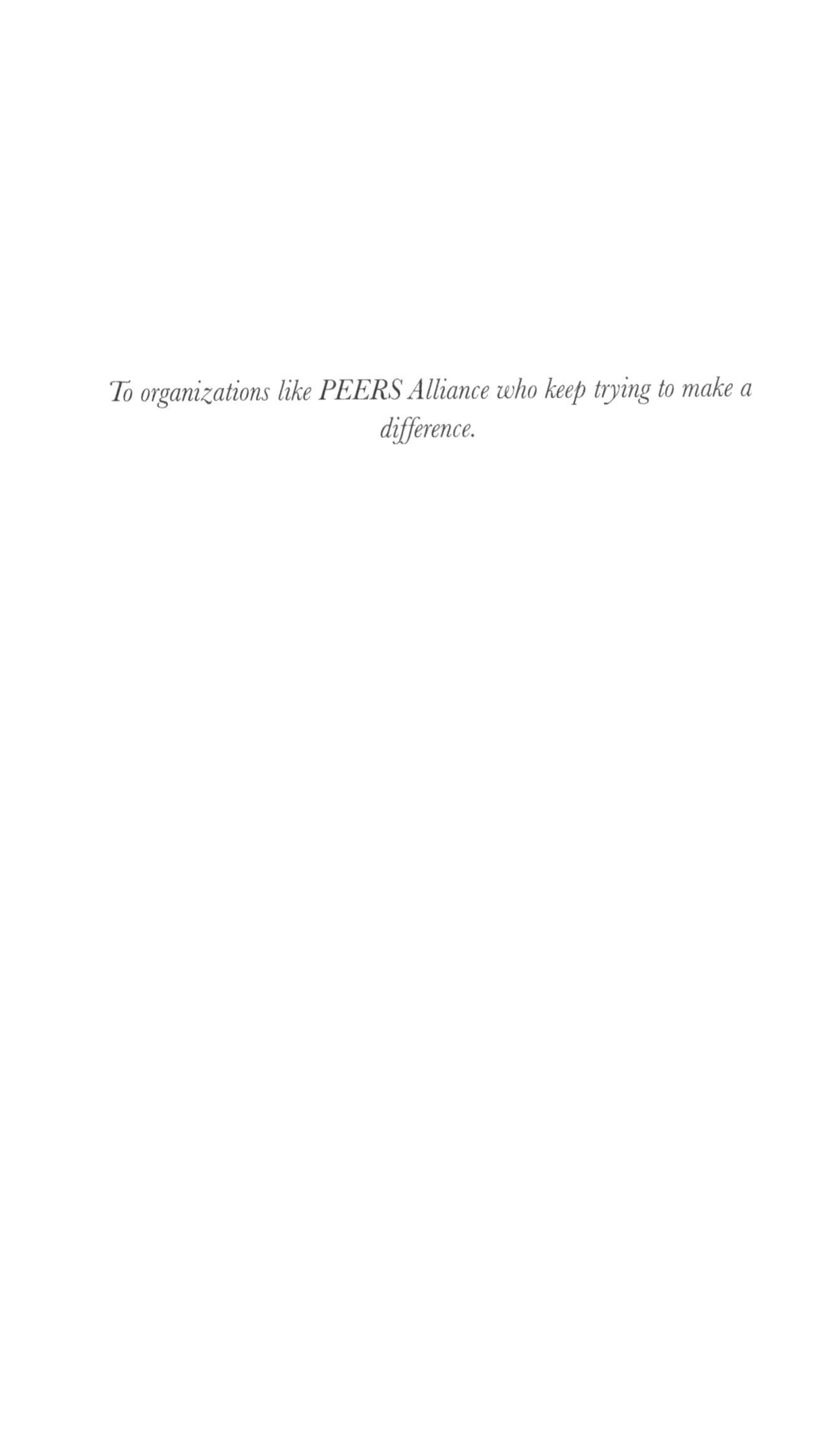

To organizations like PEERS Alliance who keep trying to make a difference.

AUTHOR'S NOTE

This is a m/m paranormal romance story about werewolves, and it's a spin-off story of my Cricket Kendall series. **Rises the Moon** can be read on it's own, and it is a completed story. However, there are brief mentions and hints of things in Cricket's series. Quentin, Nico, Helena, and Felix will also make appearances later in Cricket's series too.

Rises the Moon was previously included in the anthology *Under the Rainbow: A 2SLGBTQ+ Romance Charity Anthology for PEERS Alliance*. The anthology is no longer available.

BLURB

After taking a gap year to travel the world with his best friend, Quentin is summoned home to his father's pack and forced to attend a pack-gathering to increase the odds of finding his mate. Quentin has no interest in meeting his mate or settling down. He wants his life to be an adventure, and he wants to be free. He doesn't care about being an alpha or forming his own pack, and he dreads the idea of being forced into a soul-sucking career to support a family he doesn't even want.

But his dad's never been one to take no for an answer, so Quentin returns home with his tail tucked between his legs. When he finds out that the Evil Twins will be attending the pack-gathering too, he's more bitter than ever. Helena and Nico are pretentious, conniving sociopaths who have been intent on making Quentin's life miserable since they were kids. It doesn't help that everyone seems to think Quentin and Helena could be mates. He dodged a bullet last year by skipping the pack-gathering right after the Evil Twins turned sixteen, but now he's out of excuses. He'll have to confront them.

When Quentin and Helena are reunited for the first time in two years, they're relieved to discover they're not mates. Quentin feels like the Moon Goddess has thrown him a bone, giving him his freedom for just a little longer.

Until he comes face to face with Nico, and he's forced to question everything he always thought he knew about himself.

ONE

QUENTIN

Felix says.

My grip on the steering wheel tightens, and I keep my gaze straight ahead. I'm driving something like twenty over the speed limit, but there's no one else on the road. Not out here in bumfuck-nowhere West Texas. And even if I do pass any cops by chance, they'll most likely apologize and wish me a good fucking day after they hear my dad's name.

"We could only be so lucky." I sigh.

Felix whines and shuffles lower in his seat. Without looking, I reach over and ruffle his hair lightly. If it's painful for me to return home, I know it's a million times worse for him.

My dad's territory stretches from the border of Arizona, through the entire state of New Mexico, and everywhere in Texas west of San Antonio. At least, as far as I know. It's possible he's expanded since I left home over a year ago. Unlike most alphas, my dad doesn't run a single pack. He's in charge of dozens. I have no clue how many. However many werewolf packs live within the boundaries of his territory, I guess. I stopped asking questions about the way my dad runs things when I was thirteen and overheard some shady business deal between him and a senator.

I'm sure he has countless cops, politicians, and people with any shred of power in his pocket. And I don't want any part of that.

"How much farther?" Felix asks. He's restless, fidgeting in his seat.

I wish there was more I could do to make my beta feel better, but I'm stuck. Wincing apologetically, I tell him, "Not much. Twenty minutes, maybe?"

He nods, and I force myself to relax my grip on the wheel. We can get through this. If I don't meet my mate at this pack-gathering, I'm sure my dad will let us leave. We can go back to traveling, like we have been over the past year. Any new exotic place we can find that's thousands of miles away from my dad's territory. We just need to get through this week.

Sometimes I'm still surprised my dad let us leave at all. After Felix and I graduated last year, I asked if I could put off going to school or work for a year to travel. I argued that seeing more of the world would make me a better, stronger alpha, and that I'd get some of my restless energy out of my system and be more prepared to settle down with my mate after having a few adventures. For the first time in my life, my dad actually agreed with me.

I should have known it could never last.

When I see the sign for the ranch, I reach over to ruffle Felix's hair again to give him any ounce of comfort I can. At least we're not going *home*-home. Back to the house where I grew up in Santa Fe. My dad prefers hosting pack-gatherings out here in the middle of nowhere. This ranch is made up of several hundred acres, and we're miles away from the nearest town. There's plenty of space for wolves to run wild without the threat of being seen by humans. At least out here, Felix and I will probably get a cabin to ourselves, and my dad will be too busy barking orders at the other wolves in attendance to spend *all* his time barking orders at me.

After driving down the long, gravel driveway that leads to the main part of the ranch, we finally reach the big building where the gathering is hosted. It's a giant, sleek, modern building with five floors, appearing completely out of place in the middle of the West Texas desert. My dad can't help throwing money around even for something like this. Outside of the main building, there's a huge patio and an area for barbequing. Dozens of cabins surround the whole structure. The biggest, flashiest one is reserved for my dad, of course, and my mom, on the rare occasions she can pull herself away from her life of self-indulgence back in Santa Fe. A handful of other large cabins—just short of being considered mansions— are reserved for the stronger alphas' families of the attending packs.

"There's your dad," Felix whispers, nodding toward the side of the main building.

Nausea coils in my stomach, but I've gotta be strong. Not only for Felix, but for myself. If my dad catches a whiff of weakness from me, he'll never let me forget it.

I park in the gravel lot between a Mercedes and a Jaguar. Why these dumbasses would drive their fancy cars out *here* is beyond me, but I'm sure my dad will still say something about the 'shitty' rental Felix and I picked up from the airport this morning. Before I can brace myself or offer my beta any words of encouragement, I see my dad walking in our direc- tion. I curse under my breath, share a look with Felix, and get out of the car.

"Son," my dad barks. He exudes cold, cruel authority as he strides across the lot to meet me. I take a deep breath, hold my head high, and meet his eyes as I walk to meet him half- way. He gives me his version of a smile and holds out his hand for me to shake. "How was the trip?"

"Great." I make sure my handshake is firm, doing my best

to appear like the strong alpha he wishes I was. "Long, but everything went smooth."

He nods, sparing Felix a fleeting glance over my shoulder. His mouth dips into a slight frown before he meets my eyes again. "Most of the packs attending this year have arrived already. Come inside and see if any of these females are your mate."

It takes everything in me not to bristle at his alpha order. I'm fucking nineteen years old, yet I'm still a slave to his alpha voice. Most alphas break away from their birth packs after they graduate high school these days, either when they meet their mate or with their alpha's permission. My dad refuses to let me go until I meet my mate and complete the mating bond. Until I trade one prison sentence for another.

"I thought we could settle in first," I say, trying to make it sound like a suggestion rather than an argument. "We've been traveling for over twenty-four hours, and we're jetlagged."

My dad holds up a key to one of the cabins, and I nearly sigh in relief. When I go to grab them, he snatches them back and rumbles out a growling laugh. "Females first, and then you can settle in. After this, I won't bother you for the rest of the night."

Without another word, he turns on his heel and heads toward the main entrance of the building. I look over my shoulder at Felix, and he shrugs.

"Let's just get it over with," he whispers.

We walk side by side, following behind my dad. Felix bumps his elbow against mine, which makes me smile. I couldn't ask for a better best friend. He's been my rock for as long as I can remember. Even here and now, when I know he's hurting worse than I am, he's offering me any support he can.

The closer we get to the door, the more anxious I feel. What if my mate *is* here? What the fuck am I going to do? At least my dad leaves me alone most of the time these days. He only checks in every couple months. When I'm away, I'm a problem he can easily ignore. But if I meet my mate? I have no doubt my dad will push me into taking a soul-sucking job in one of the bigger cities in his territory where he'll *always* have some semblance of control over me. And how long will it be before my mate wants to have pups? Werewolves always have kids young. I don't want any at all, but I don't see how I'll ever get away with that. Especially if my mate is a female alpha or the least bit power-hungry.

I don't know what's worse. Continuing living under my dad's thumb with the restrictions I'm at least familiar with, or being tied to a mate I want nothing to do with and no way of knowing what to expect in the future.

"Hurry up," my dad barks at us over his shoulder, using his alpha voice.

Just one week, I remind myself. We just have to get through one fucking week, and then we can try to escape again.

TWO

QUENTIN

Seventeen girls stand lined up against a wall, each of them staring at me like a hungry predator. They're all unmated, all somewhere between the age of sixteen and twenty-two. I love hooking up with hot girls just as much as the next guy, but watching these girls preen for me like this makes my stomach turn. Felix stands at my shoulder, but none of the girls spare him a glance. They only care to see if *I'm* their mate. The great Alpha Peterson's youngest son.

It makes me fucking livid. Nobody here knows that Felix is mateless—that he doesn't have a mate mark. My dad has made sure to keep that a secret because it would be such a *disgrace* if anyone knew his alpha son's beta was *defective*. Every time we're around wolves, Felix has to make sure his wrists are covered. Today, he's wearing a long-sleeve shirt even though it's hot as balls outside.

Still, these girls don't know that. For all they know, Felix could be their fated mate just as easily as I could. It's obvious none of them care about what a mate mark is *supposed* to mean. It's all about what they can gain from being tied to a powerful wolf like they assume I am.

Filled with rage and disgust at the blatant desperation of

the unmated females, I'm forced to approach them one by one to compare the marks on our wrists. I'm fairly certain nobody here is my mate—I would be able to feel it, right? That makes it easier to go down the line, meeting each girl's eyes before comparing our marks.

When it's over, I breathe out a sigh of relief and turn to my dad. He can't be mad that I didn't find my mate here. It's not like I have any control over this.

He hands me a key and grunts in disapproval. I couldn't really give a shit how he feels. I just wanna get to our cabin and chill for the night. Before I can grab the key and make a break for it with Felix, my dad growls at me.

"It's probably for the best that none of these females are your mate. None of them are very strong or high-ranking," he says. While I agree that I'm glad none of them are my mate, I want to roll my eyes at his reason for thinking it's best. He gives me his cold version of a smile and adds, "The Kallis pack will be here tomorrow. We've always thought there was a good chance their girl Helena could be your mate."

I recoil. I always try to keep my emotions in check in front of my dad, but this time, I can't control my reaction. My dad scowls, and I quickly rush out, "I doubt that. We hate each other. The twins—"

"Enough," he says with his alpha voice. My mouth snaps shut. I wordlessly follow my dad outside, Felix hot on my heels. Once we're out of view and hearing range of any nearby wolves, my dad turns to me with a snarl. "Do not disrespect me in front of the packs. Ever. You know better."

Even though I feel myself shrinking internally—even though his words bring back memories of all the times he hit me as a kid to teach me a lesson—I keep my eyes on his and make sure my posture makes me appear strong and confident.

"I'm sorry," I say. "I meant no disrespect."

He points his finger at me, centimeters from my face, and growls, "You'll be back here in the morning, bright and early to greet the Kallis girl. And you'll have a fucking smile on your face. Not that grimace you were wearing inside with those other females."

With that, he tosses the cabin key at my feet and storms away, back into the main building. The second he's out of sight, I take a deep, shaky breath. Felix scrambles to pick up the key from the ground, grabbing my elbow to lead me to our rental car.

"Come on," he says softly. "Let's get our stuff and find our cabin."

I SNORT WHEN I OPEN THE DOOR, TOSSING MY DUFFEL DOWN. We're in one of the smaller cabins on the outskirts of the property, typically left for low-ranking wolves. I'm sure it's supposed to be an insult to me, but I'd much rather be *here*, as far from my dad as I can get.

"Does your dad really think this is a punishment?" Felix laughs, flopping back onto the couch. Dust goes flying everywhere, making him cough before he shoots me a grin. "We've stayed in way smaller, shittier places the past year. Shit, we even get our own bedrooms here."

One of the conditions my dad gave me when it came to traveling was that I'd have to pay my own way, despite the fact that he's filthy rich and I have a trust fund. I'm not allowed to touch my trust until I complete the mating bond with my mate, anyway. I'm sure he thought forcing me and Felix to struggle financially on our own would make us return home sooner, but we loved every second of our borrowed freedom. We picked up odd jobs all the time and hunted for food in our wolf forms when things were too desolate. I'd spend my whole life living like that if it meant never having to deal with my dad again.

"Probably a hot shower too." My lips curve into a smile.

Joking around with Felix like everything's normal helps me feel a million times better.

At least for a moment, until I remember I have to see the Evil Twins in the morning.

The Kallises aren't one of the packs under my dad's thumb, but they've been friends with my parents for as long as I can remember. Their territory takes up every part of Texas that my dad doesn't control. While Mr. and Mrs. Kallis have always seemed nice, and nowhere near as shady as my dad, their kids are fucking awful.

Helena and Nico are a couple years younger than me and Felix, so they must be seventeen by now. I haven't seen the demons since a few months before I graduated high school and took off to travel the world. Helena *is* a strong alpha. I've always known it. Our parents have been saying our whole lives how perfect it would be if we turned out to be mates.

"Fuck, Felix." I sigh, feeling like something's clawing at my chest. "What if Helena is my mate? What am I going to do?"

He sits up on the couch, grimacing as he shrugs at me. "Fall madly in love, complete your bond, get married, and have babies?"

I snort and flip him off, and he cracks a grin.

"Honestly," he says. "She's probably made Nico her beta by now, and yeah, they're unbearable. But they don't live in your dad's territory. We could go live in Houston with them. Maybe they won't even wanna stay in Texas or expand their parents' pack. It could be a fresh start somewhere new. It's not ideal, but it wouldn't be the worst thing."

He's right. It wouldn't be the worst thing. That doesn't mean the thought of being mated to Helena doesn't make me want to claw my eyes out. All the times she and her demon-twin made my life miserable when we were growing up flash through my mind. Our families used to go on vacation together, and the Kallises always came to visit us in Santa Fe. The twins would follow me and Felix around constantly.

They'd spy on us and snitch on us for every little thing—my dad always waited until the Kallises went home to punish me, but I'll never be able to forget how smug the twins looked whenever they ratted me out. When they got older, Helena would challenge me every time we reunited, just to prove she's the stronger wolf between us. The twins have always loved to rub their successes in my face, always set on proving how superior they are. How much stronger, smarter, and all-around better they are than me.

Worst of all, they've always gone out of their way to make Felix feel inferior too. They pick on him, push him, call him names. And I can never forgive them for that. Felix says the twins don't bother him as much as they bother me, but I don't believe him. I can take it, and he doesn't deserve that shit. Not from anyone. Not after everything he's been through.

"Why don't you shower first?" I ask, trying to change the subject. A shower and some sleep sound like heaven right about now.

Felix nods. When he goes to stand up from the couch, his stomach grumbles loudly. He gives me a sheepish smile, and we laugh. Fuck, when's the last time we ate? During our layover in New York? How many hours ago was that?

"I'll go back to the main building to grab some food for us," I offer. There's a cafeteria on the second floor, and there's bound to be plenty of leftovers. We only missed dinnertime by about an hour.

"I can go with you."

"No." I shake my head. "You should stay here and shower. I'll be quick, and I doubt my dad will bother with me anymore tonight."

I can see he wants to argue with me and insist on coming along, and he knows I'll never use my alpha voice on him, so there's not much I can do to stop him. But he must see it in my eyes—how guilty I feel for dragging him along with me, and how badly I wish I could do a better job of protecting him. He nods slowly and says, "Okay, Q. I'll shower and then check to see if we're lucky enough to have any cable or Wi-Fi."

"Man, we'll be living like kings tonight." I grin.

We laugh, and I take a deep breath before heading out to find us some food.

THREE

QUENTIN

"Thanks, Miss Lucy."

I lift the bags filled to the brim with food containers and cans of Dr. Pepper. Miss Lucy is an older, lower-ranking wolf who's worked for my dad forever. Long before I was born. She's always been a sweetheart to me, even though she's afraid of my dad. When I was a kid, she would slip me sweets whenever I saw her, and she still tries to go out of her way for me when I see her now. The second I walked into the kitchen in search of something to eat, she started putting together enough food to last me and Felix for days.

She waves me off, giving me a gentle smile. "Tell Felix I say hello, just in case I don't get a chance to see the two of you much this week."

"Will do," I say.

Making my way downstairs, I've got a smile on my face for the first time since I stepped off the plane in this godforsaken state. Felix will be stoked when he smells the burgers, fries, onion rings, and apple pie Lucy loaded me up with. It's all the greasy American food we've missed the most over the past few months.

The first floor of the main building is still crowded with

members of the packs. Everyone's standing around, talking and mingling excitedly. I spot my dad weaving between groups, keeping an eye on everything. I hold my breath and stealthily make my way to the exit, hoping he won't stop me even if he happens to notice my presence.

Outside, I let myself take a breath. There's still a chance my dad could come outside behind me or track me down later tonight, but it's not very likely. Not after I willingly followed his demands today. It's just a short walk to the cabin Felix and I are sharing, and then I can try to enjoy the rest of our night in peace.

The sun is just starting to set, bathing the desert in a soft, pink light. If I didn't have so many bad memories of growing up around here, I might think it was pretty. Instead, it just makes me feel really fucking sad and hopeless. Walking through the parking lot, I catch a familiar scent and slow my steps.

Helena Kallis stands beside a fancy black Land Rover, her dark brown eyes brimming over with judgment. She looks just like I remember. Tall with small curves and slim hips, long, straight black hair, thick eyebrows, a long, elegant nose, and full lips. I thought the twins were coming tomorrow. Why couldn't I just have one night with the illusion of peace where I could pretend me and Felix could spend our lives traveling the world, carefree and happy?

"Hello, stranger." Helena sneers at me.

"Thought you weren't getting here until tomorrow," I grumble.

She shrugs, walking around to the back of the vehicle to open the trunk. "Nico and I decided to drive up tonight." I stand completely still, watching her pull four large suitcases out of the back. She huffs and turns to glare at me. "Gee, sure would be nice if there were a strong, egotistical alpha around here to help a damsel out."

Her snark snaps me out of my frozen state, and I furrow

my eyebrows as I look around the parking lot in an exaggerated manner. "Damsel? I don't see your brother anywhere."

"Ha-ha." She rolls her eyes, waving her hand at the suitcases. "Come on. Let's just get this over with and compare our marks. Then can you please help me carry these into our cabin?"

I bite my tongue and force myself to keep my mouth shut. The attitude and fucking entitlement haven't changed a bit. Guess it was stupid of me to hope the Evil Twins might have changed or grown up to be halfway decent over the past year and a half. But if I say anything in retaliation or refuse to help her, there's no doubt my dad will hear about it. If I'm lucky, *I'll* take the punishment for my bad behavior.

Unfortunately, it's more likely that Felix will end up being my dad's punching bag while I'm forced to watch under the suffocating blanket of his alpha order.

The only silver lining is that after seeing Helena again, I'm fairly certain she's not my mate. Just like I didn't feel it with any of the females inside, I don't feel it with her now either.

"Sure." I sigh. Every step closer to her feels like torture. "But can we make it quick? Felix is waiting for me."

Helena purses her lips. "Right. Your precious beta."

A growl slips out, and I don't bother disguising it as I settle a glare on her. Helena might be pretty on the outside, but she's still fucking poison on the inside. I set my bags of food down gently and hold my wrist out, waiting for her to do the same.

She meets my eyes, slowly holding her wrist out, and then we look down at the same time.

Our marks don't match. Not even close. It takes everything in me not to breathe out a sigh of relief.

"Thank the goddess." Helena laughs. My eyes snap up to meet hers in surprise, and she snorts. "You didn't think I *wanted* to be your mate, did you?"

"I never presume to know anything that goes on in your head."

A smile blooms on her face. It's not a look I've ever seen on her, and it's fucking creepy. I think she might be genuinely smiling at me. "It's kind of anticlimactic, isn't it?" she asks. "After all the crap our parents always said while we were growing up."

Shrugging, I pick up two of her suitcases. "I knew we weren't mates."

Helena laughs again before grabbing the other two bags. Hearing her laugh is even weirder than seeing her smile. Was she seriously only being a bitch to me all these years because she was worried she'd be stuck with me as a mate? Should I be offended?

Shaking the thoughts off, I decide it doesn't matter what her reasons were. The twins have spent years making my life more miserable than it already was. And I seriously doubt Nico's going to randomly start being nice to me when he hears I'm not his sister's mate.

I'm not surprised when Helena leads me to one of the fancier cabins near the main building. It's only a two-bedroom, so I assume she and Nico have it to themselves instead of sharing with their parents. It makes sense since Helena's a powerful alpha, and the twins are of age now.

"You make Nico your beta yet?" I ask, mildly curious.

"Yep. On our sixteenth birthday." She glances at me over her shoulder. "Our parents are pretty traditional. We can't all be rebels and choose our betas when we're ten years old."

"Not like you would have chosen anyone else though. So, what's the point in waiting?"

She stops right outside the door and gives me a look. Like she's seeing me the first time. "How could you possibly know if you were making the right decision when you were so young?"

I don't know what compels me to say anything. All the

years I've known Helena and Nico, I've never really *talked* to them. Not about anything important. Maybe it's from the relief of knowing she's not my mate or the hope that maybe she'll be halfway decent whenever we interact from now on.

"Did you know I made Felix my beta an hour after I met him? If that. At the time, it was the only way I could think to protect him. I've never regretted it or second-guessed my decision. I might have wished I could do better for him, but no. I'd never choose anyone else."

Her eyebrows raise, and she opens her mouth like she's going to say something. A loud crash from inside the cabin distracts us, and Helena throws the door open to rush inside.

"Nico? Everything okay?" she asks.

I barely register her voice, or the fact that I never thought to wonder where Nico was or why *he* wasn't the one to help his sister with their bags. The only thing I can focus on is the intoxicating scent filling their cabin. It's familiar and not-familiar, somehow, and I flare my nostrils to inhale as much of it as I can.

"What *is* that?" I ask, growling quietly as I step in behind her. Whatever it is, I'm pretty sure I want to roll around in it until I can never smell anything else again.

Footsteps in the hallway make me look up, and I meet Nico's eyes. Only, he's not the Nico I remember. Not the spoiled, pretentious brat that makes up the second half of the Evil Twins. No, he's *Nico*. So fucking pretty and enticing. Taller than I remember, so he's only a couple inches shorter than me. Lean muscles, messy curls falling into his caramel brown eyes, light stubble along his sharp jaw, and thick eyebrows, a straight nose and full lips like his sister—except those features are a million times better on his face.

I walk over to him slowly, unable to blink or look away as I stare at him in awe and wonder if I've lost my mind. Is that his scent driving me crazy? Fuck, it is. Like vanilla, cinnamon, and sugar. If I lick him, will he taste like that too? The thought nearly makes me groan.

Nico growls softly, his gaze dropping from mine so he can slowly and sensually drag his eyes up and down my body. I feel myself stand up straighter, and my cock goes rock fucking hard. When he bites his lip and glances up at me through his impossibly long lashes, I lose it. I drop the suitcases I'm still holding and grab his arm, pulling him closer while turning his wrist over to inspect his mark.

His mark matches mine. There's no doubt in my mind, even before I hold my wrist up to see our marks side by side. My wolf is beyond elated, practically screaming at me. *Mate, mate, mate. Mine, mine, mine.*

A split second of clarity hits me. I close my eyes and shake my head, dropping Nico's arm as I take a step backwards.

"What?" I ask, my heart racing and my stomach flipping. I can't tell if I'm excited or just panicking. His scent and the way he *looks* and the fact that he's somehow my fucking mate are making me feel lightheaded. "I don't understand. *How* can we be mates? Holy shit. I'm straight. I don't…"

I trail off when a thought hits me. What is my dad going to think about this? What is he going to do? He'll be furious. It doesn't matter that Nico's from a strong pack with alpha parents. My dad's said enough shit about me and Felix being gay—despite the fact that our relationship has never been anything other than platonic—that I know he won't be okay with this. He'll do whatever he can to ruin it.

Nico's lips move, but I don't hear what he says. My ears are ringing while I stare at him, speechless and terrified. Would my dad hurt him? He hurts Felix to get back at me. Would he really be so ballsy as to hurt Nico too? Even knowing who his family is? Fuck, just the thought makes me dizzy. If I can't protect myself or Felix, how am I ever going to protect my mate?

"I—" My voice comes out scratchy, so I clear my throat as

I shake my head and back away slowly. "I have to go. Felix is waiting for me."

Hurt flashes in Nico's eyes. Only for a split second, but it's enough for me to want to drop to my knees and beg for his forgiveness. I quickly look away before he can tempt me any further. I need to process the fact that my mate is a *male* and figure out what I'm going to do about my dad.

Helena shouts something at me about being an asshole, but I shove past her anyway. I barely have the presence of mind to remember the bags of food I left by her SUV, and I quickly snatch them up before running back to my cabin as fast as I can.

I barge through the door, faintly registering that Felix is sitting on the couch with our laptop on the coffee table in front of him. He looks up at me with a smile, wet hair falling into his eyes.

"Hey—" he cuts himself off, standing up in alarm when he sees the look on my face. "What's wrong? What happened?"

Shaking my head at a complete loss, I growl mournfully and say, "Nico. Fucking *Nico.*"

"You ran into the twins?" Felix asks, furrowing his eyebrows in confusion.

I set the food on the tiny breakfast table beside the front door, shaking my hands to try and expel some of the chaotic energy coursing through my body. "No. Yes. Fuck, man. Helena isn't my mate. *Nico* is. Nico's my fucking mate."

Felix's jaw drops in shock, and he stares at me like he's waiting for me to tell him I'm joking around. When I feel tears well up in the corners of my eyes and a pitiful whine escapes my throat, I tug my hands roughly through my hair.

"Fuck. What am I going to do? It fucking *kills* me whenever my dad hurts you because of me. If he does that shit to Nico? I don't—I can't handle it. What is he going to do when he finds out that my mate is a guy? He'll say my mark is defective. He'll say—"

Felix growls and slaps his hand over my mouth. It shuts me up long enough for him to pull me into a tight hug. I hug him back, another whine and a sob escaping me.

"Forget your dad," Felix says. "He's fucking garbage. We can worry about him later, alright? Without thinking about how your dad is going to react, tell me how you feel. Are you…happy that Nico's your mate?"

It's hard to think rationally or to stop worrying about my dad, but I try to settle down and think about my feelings. The first words that come out of my mouth are, "I like girls."

Felix snorts, shoving me back and giving me an amused smile. "Sexuality is a spectrum, dude. And that doesn't answer my question."

I shrug, feeling embarrassed but also really fucking giddy when I remember Nico's scent and the way he looked after reuniting for the first time in so long. "It's like…I've seen Nico a million times, right? And never thought anything except that he was an evil little shit. But then today, he just…he looks *so good*. And his scent—fuck. I know it's probably the mate bond making me feel like this, but I want him. So bad. I just wanna protect him and make him happy, and I don't think I can do that."

"Sure you can." Felix grins, reaching up to ruffle my hair. "You're the best alpha in the world. Once you complete your bond with Nico, your dad won't have any power over you. We can take off and start fresh with our new pack, and you can spend your whole life being a sappy shit trying to make Nico happy."

A laugh rumbles in my chest. It was less than an hour ago that Felix was giving me practically the same advice in case Helena turned out to be my mate. But maybe he's right. Once I complete my mating bond, my dad can't use his alpha voice on me. Felix and I can form a new pack with Nico and

Helena. I don't even care where they want to settle and claim a territory. As long as it's not here.

"I might have already fucked up," I say, my shoulders slumping. "I freaked out and ran away when I realized we were mates. He probably doesn't want anything to do with me." Another thought occurs to me, and panic spreads through my chest. "What if he thinks he's straight too? What if he doesn't wanna be with me just because I'm a guy? What about *his* parents? They can't be as bad as my dad, but they're still pretty traditional."

Felix pulls me into a headlock and ruffles my hair until I laugh and push him away. He huffs at me, a crooked smile curving at his lips. "Stop worrying so much. It's supposed to be fate, right? Just try to chill the fuck out, dude. Go take a shower and eat something, and then we can make a plan for you to woo your mate properly."

With all the excitement, I've completely forgotten about the food and how long it's been since I've eaten. My stomach rumbles on cue, and Felix shoves me toward the bathroom and promises to heat up the food while I shower.

While I wait for the water to warm up, I take deep, calming breaths. Felix is right. He and I have always trusted each other, and that hasn't changed just because I've found my mate. After I woo Nico and make him realize that we're meant to be together, everything else will work itself out. It has to.

FOUR

NICO

I BRUSH MY FINGERS BACK AND FORTH ACROSS THE MATE MARK on my wrist, a low whine getting caught in my throat. Every minute that passes while I wait for my mark to turn black is torture. It feels like my heart is shattering over and over, making every breath I take that much more difficult.

The bedroom door crashes open, and the light switches on. I squint at the sudden brightness, turning to glare at my twin.

"What are you doing, Nico?" Helena asks exasperatedly.

"Nothing." I growl, pulling my blanket up over my head so I can go back to mourning in peace.

I listen to her footsteps as she crosses the room, and she sits on the edge of my bed. When she gently places her hand on my shoulder, I swallow the lump in my throat and try to blink away the tears threatening to form in my eyes.

"Nothing, my ass." She growls. "I can hear you whining and whimpering from my bedroom. Have you slept at all?"

Shaking my head, I peek my head out of my blanket and glance at the tacky, digital alarm clock on the bedside table. This is supposed to be one of the nicer cabins on the property, but so many of the features are horribly outdated. When I register that it's just after four in the morning, another whimper leaves my mouth. It's been nearly eight hours since Quentin ran away from me.

"Can't sleep," I whisper, shrugging. I can't even look at my sister. I don't want to see the pity on her face. "Just waiting for him to make the rejection official."

Helena grunts and yanks my arm out from under the blankets, glaring down at my wrist. She gives me another exasperated look. "Nico, you're being ridiculous. Let's just go talk to him."

"No!" I sit up in the bed, snatching my hand back and cradling it against my chest.

Just the thought of facing Quentin again after the way he reacted makes me want to throw up. When I first saw him earlier, I swear there were a few seconds where he looked at me like I was his whole world. He looked at me the way I've been wishing almost my entire life he'd look at me. And then it all came crashing down when he literally ran away. Even knowing he's my mate, he still chose stupid Felix over me. Just like he always has.

"Why not?" Helena asks. "You're just sitting here, feeling lousy and miserable. We can clear this up. And if he keeps acting like an asshole, I have an excuse to kick his ass."

"Seriously, Lena?" I stare at her incredulously. "How can you even suggest I go talk to him? You saw his face when he ran out of here earlier. He was disgusted by the fact that he's my mate. He clearly doesn't want anything to do with me. I just wish he'd officially end it already. Get it over with."

"Goddess, you're dramatic." My twin rolls her eyes. "He's not going to reject you. Even a himbo like Quentin Peterson knows how dangerous and risky it is to reject your mate. And anyway, he didn't look disgusted. Stunned, maybe, but not disgusted. You heard what he said. The stupid boy thought he was straight until a few hours ago."

Which doesn't make sense at all. Hasn't he been fucking

Felix for *years?* I've always been under the assumption that they were together, and just really terrible at hiding their relationship. Helena and I even heard Quentin's dad insinuate there was something romantic between Quentin and his beta.

It's been a sore spot for me since I was eight years old. The first time I ever met Quentin, I completely fell in love with him. Yeah, it was probably just stupid puppy love since we were so young, but my feelings for him have only gotten stronger as I've grown up. Every time our families got together, I'd follow him around like a lovesick idiot. I'd ask him a million questions so I could learn everything about him, and I'd brag incessantly about all the things I liked and was good at in the hopes it would impress him and make him like me. For the first year I knew Quentin, he never seemed to mind much. He put up with me and Helena, at least.

But then *Felix* moved in with the Petersons. Helena and I were eight, and Quentin and Felix were ten. When I found out that Quentin made Felix his beta, I was so full of rage and jealousy. Felix is everything I'm not. He's nice, funny, sweet, smart, and Quentin *likes* him. He could barely tolerate me before Felix came into the picture, but after? Everything I did always seemed to annoy and infuriate Quentin. He never cared to get to know me. Never cared about anything I did or said. He'd get mad at me for following him around, for so much as *talking* to him. Around Felix though, he's like a totally different person. So happy and full of life. He's never once looked at me the way he's looked at Felix.

"I know what you're thinking," Helena says. "But maybe we were wrong about him and Felix. Quentin sounded genuine when he said he was straight, and he said something weird to me outside just before that when he was helping me with our bags. Something about making Felix his beta to protect him."

I make a face at her. *Maybe* he and Felix really are just friends, but it's still hard to believe. Especially after all the times I've seen them hug, hold hands, or nuzzle each other. They've always been so fucking *affectionate* with each other. My dad's never been like that with his beta. Goddess, Helena and I aren't even like that, and we're twins.

"How is that supposed to make me feel better?" I scoff. "If he's not rejecting me for Felix, he's rejecting me because I have a dick."

Helena crosses her arms, a look of determination on her face. I brace myself for an alpha order from her, tensing up in preparation. I know she's going to insist I go talk to Quentin. She just doesn't get how this feels. How devastating it is to find out for *sure* that the guy I've spent my entire childhood and adolescence pining after is my fated mate, only to have him reject me within seconds of realizing it. Knowing my parents were hoping *Helena* would be Quentin's mate makes every-thing worse. I feel like I can't even talk to them. They'll be disappointed whether Quentin accepts or rejects me.

"Let's go talk to Quentin," Helena says in her alpha voice. Just like I knew she would. "Don't let him hide from this."

I breathe angrily out of my nose and gesture at the stupid, digital alarm clock. "It's four in the morning. He's probably asleep."

"Who cares? This is more important than His Highness's beauty sleep."

After she uses her alpha voice again to hurry me along, I grudgingly get up and pull on a pair of sweatpants and a hoodie. It's blazing hot during the day, but it gets so chilly at night out here in the middle of the desert. Guess I'm gonna have to get used to the cold soon though, since Lena and I are moving to Washington for school in the fall.

"Ugh, how much farther?" I ask, tripping over another rock. Even with my enhanced eyesight, it's too fucking dark outside to see shit.

"Cabin number 106," Helena mumbles, squinting at her

phone screen. "I thought he'd be in one of the bigger cabins like us."

It takes us nearly ten minutes of stumbling through the dark before we reach the cabins on the outskirts of the housing area. Somehow, I always forget how big Alpha Peterson's territory is. Just seeing all the packs who attend his pack-gatherings is staggering, and I know it's still nowhere close to the number of packs he controls.

My heart jumps into my throat when I see the small, wooden placard with the number 106 on it, and I force myself to take a step closer. The cabins way back here are tiny—they're practically shacks. If I thought some of the features in mine and Helena's cabin were outdated, I can't even imagine what these ones look like inside.

The unmistakable sound of moaning coming from inside Quentin's cabin stops me in my tracks. Is he…? No. *No.* Not only did he run away from me earlier, clearly if not officially rejecting me, but now he's fucking someone else? I taste bile in the back of my throat, and I feel so dizzy that I know I'm only seconds from fainting.

"Stay right here," Helena orders. I sway on my feet, wincing as I bring my hands up to cover my ears. It doesn't help at all. I can still hear moaning. My sister stomps the rest of the way to the cabin, banging loudly on the front door.

A few seconds later, the front porch light flicks on, and Felix pokes his head outside. He rubs his hand over his eyes and stares at Helena in confusion before a bright, smug smile blooms across his face. He says something to Helena, but my brain is too focused on the fact that I can still hear someone moaning inside. Someone clearly male. Is Quentin fucking someone else? What, to prove to himself that he's straight?

I don't even realize I'm crying until Helena snarls at Felix. "You'd better tell me what the fuck is going on inside your cabin before I beat your ass and then hunt down your fucking alpha. Is he seriously with someone else right now, *knowing* my brother's his mate?"

Felix's eyes widen, and he quickly shakes his head as he steps further outside and closes the door behind him. "No, no. Fuck, Q's going to be so embarrassed. He's, uh, he's been watching porn all night?"

"What?" Helena practically shouts. Felix winces, peering over her shoulder to look at me.

"Listen, it's really late. Or early? Why don't you guys come in? Just…promise to be quiet, please. Q hasn't slept in something like forty-eight hours, and he finally passed out. I must have dozed off before he did, otherwise I would have turned the fucking TV off already. I'm honestly surprised your banging on the door didn't wake him up like it did me."

Helena looks at me, waiting for my decision. Which is really rich, considering she's the one who made me come here in the first place. I glare at her and hesitantly walk the last few steps up to the front door. I just…need to know. See for myself if Felix is telling the truth. I don't get why Quentin would stay up all night watching porn, but that's got to be a million times better than him hooking up with somebody else.

Felix opens the door wide for me, giving me a huge grin. "After you, Luna."

I bristle and turn to glare at him. Is he teasing me? It's always so hard to tell with him. At least he's acknowledging that I'm Quentin's mate. Luna is the nickname male alphas usually give their mates. That has to mean something, right?

Under the bright porch light, I get my first good look at Quentin's beta. He's just like I remember. Slightly taller than me with broad shoulders and a lot more muscle tone, wavy blond hair, icy blue eyes, and an impossibly charming smile. He's the complete opposite of me, which has always made Quentin's preference for his company sting that much more. Swallowing back an insult or sarcastic remark, I run my eyes over Felix critically. He looks…disheveled. His clothes are rumpled, and there are bags under his eyes.

Taking a deep breath, I ignore the way my heart's racing in my chest and step into the cabin. Quentin's scent hits me right away. It's like sunshine, oranges, and a field of wildflowers. I've always been obsessed with his scent. It's so calming and happy, but it's never been so strong or driven me completely insane the way it has today.

After taking several deep breaths, filling my lungs with his scent, I look around the small cabin and find Quentin passed out on the couch. My heart stutters painfully. He looks even more disheveled than Felix. His light brown hair is a mess, sticking out all over the place, his clothes are beyond wrinkled, and he's slumped over sideways in a position that looks extremely uncomfortable. But even like this, he's so beautiful. The most beautiful person I've ever seen in my life.

"Goddess, sorry." Felix laughs awkwardly, walking over to grab the TV remote from the coffee table. I'd completely forgotten about the porn thing as soon as I smelled and saw Quentin. I look up just in time to see two ripped guys fucking on the screen before Felix turns it off.

"So, you're telling me that Quentin's been watching gay porn all night?" my sister hisses, narrowing her eyes. "To what? Convince himself he's actually straight? Or to see if he can stomach the thought of having sex with a guy?"

"What? No!" Felix says, sounding offended. He frowns at her, checks to see if Quentin is still asleep, and then turns to me. "He's not upset you're his mate or that you're a guy, if that's what you're worried about. He came back here last night, completely freaking out that he wasn't gonna be able to protect you or be a good enough mate for you. I was *trying* to help him come up with some ideas to win you over, but he was practically feral by that point after going so long without sleep and after being emotionally drained from dealing with his dad. He got it in his head that he needed to learn everything he could about, uh, gay sex. So that he'd be good at it for you."

Felix is blushing by the time he finishes speaking, and so am I. My entire body feels flushed, and I turn to look down at Quentin with a quiet, breathless laugh.

"That's stupid," Helena says.

"I never said he wasn't an idiot." Felix laughs. "I just don't want you guys thinking he didn't have good intentions. I'm pretty sure he was gonna go ask you out for breakfast this morning."

My heart keeps jumping around my chest, and my wolf is practically jumping up and down in excitement inside of me. If Felix is telling the truth, Quentin's *not* going to reject me. I'm so full of relief that I can't even be mad at him for running away from me earlier. Goddess, I just want to wake him up and beg him to tell me he wants to be with me.

But if he hasn't slept in almost two days, I need to let him sleep. It'll be torture waiting for him to wake up, but I'll do it. I'll wait. My fingers twitch with the urge to reach out and brush his soft brown hair out of his eyes, and to find a blanket to cover him up with. Would it be too weird for me to sit here and watch him sleep while I wait to talk to him? I can't bear the thought of walking away now that I know there's a chance he'll accept me as his mate.

A notebook on the ground next to the couch catches my eye. It's partially opened like it was dropped there, and there's a pencil a few inches away. I glance quickly at Quentin before crouching down to grab the notebook, and I flip to the page it was opened to.

The first thing I see is a drawing of me. My breath catches in my throat, and my eyes widen as I lightly brush my finger over it. The detail is amazing, and it looks so realistic. I can't believe he was able to draw this with a simple pencil. Goddess, I didn't even know he could draw, period. There are a few other drawings scattered around the page in between sections of writing. Drawings of our shared mate mark, of my hand and wrist, and several of just my eyes. It's the sweetest, most heartwarming thing I've ever seen.

When I finally focus on reading the words on the pages, I laugh quietly in surprise. And maybe a little embarrassment. There's a section with tips for giving blowjobs, a list of the highest rated lubes to use, and an entire how-to section of how to have sex with a guy. As a top *and* as a bottom. Flipping through the notebook, I find at least half a dozen pages like this—covered in sex advice and drawings of me. Just *reading* it is making me hard. I can't believe he spent all night thinking about this and doing all this research. Even if his research mostly consisted of watching porn.

There are also random questions scribbled in between everything. Things like: 'What is Nico's favorite color?' 'Does Nico want kids?' 'Does Nico like flowers?' 'What does Nico want to study in school?' It adds a level of sweetness and tenderness to the pages, showing proof that he's interested in *me*. Fucking me, learning more about me, getting to know me better. Sure, we've known each other most of our lives, but we were never really friends. There are still a million things we don't know about each other.

"You weren't supposed to see that."

I jump and drop the notebook at the sound of Quentin's voice, turning to stare at him guiltily. He's watching me with half-lidded eyes and a tiny smile. Having his attention on me and knowing he just caught me majorly invading his privacy makes my heart thud painfully in my chest.

"I'm sorry," I say. Only, my voice comes out sounding like a pathetic whimper, and I realize I'm still crying like a baby. Oh, goddess. This is *not* how I want him to see me after everything. I don't want to give him an excuse to run away again!

"Shh, it's alright. You've got nothing to be sorry about," Quentin whispers soothingly. He reaches out to gently grab my wrist, pulling me toward him. "Come here. Lie down with me."

Feeling like my brain is going to combust, I slowly climb up onto the couch and stretch out beside him so we're lying chest to chest. He pulls me close, wrapping one of his muscular arms around my waist while throwing one of his legs over mine. An embarrassing giggle slips out of my mouth when he tucks my head under his chin and starts nuzzling my hair.

"You smell so good," he says with a growl. I force myself to stay still and keep my mouth shut. Anything I say right now is bound to be humiliating. Quentin has never touched me. Like, ever. Maybe a handshake or a grudgingly-friendly pat on the shoulder, but never anything like this. Lying with him and being this close is a million times better than I ever imagined it could be. I never want it to end. Quentin sighs against my hair and asks, "What time is it?"

"Almost four-thirty," Felix says. His voice makes me tense up. As soon as I found Quentin's notebook, I completely forgot he and Helena were still in the room.

Quentin hums and rubs his hand over my back. "You get any sleep last night?"

It takes me a second to realize he's talking to me. "Not really."

"He's been up all night, whining and pouting about you rejecting him." Helena growls.

Ugh, goddess. I know she feels protective of me, but does she really have to embarrass me by saying that out loud? All I've ever wanted was for Quentin to like me and think I'm cool.

"That's never gonna happen." Quentin growls again, his voice sending shivers down my spine. The good kind of shivers. He lifts his hand to tilt my chin up, pulling his head far enough back to look down and meet my eyes. "I'm sorry I freaked out last night, but I swear I never considered rejecting you for one second."

"Okay." I swallow the lump in my throat, feeling my wolf relax inside of me. When Quentin keeps staring at me, like he's waiting for me to say something else, I feel my cheeks flush and let out a nervous laugh. "I'm never going to reject you either. I've been hoping you were my mate since I was seven years old."

His forest green eyes spark with surprise and happiness, and a blinding-white smile spreads across his face. I can't even find it in myself to feel embarrassed about admitting that. Having him look at me this way is more than worth it.

"Let's get some sleep, okay?" Quentin leans down to kiss my forehead, brushing his hand through my hair before wrapping his arm around my waist again. "I'll take you out to breakfast in a few hours and make it up to you for last night."

I nod, silently hoping he'll give me a real kiss. And then I start internally panicking. If he kisses me, he'll know I have pretty much zero experience. Not with kissing, and definitely not with sex. He took all those notes and watched all that porn, probably assuming I'd know everything or already have sexual preferences. But I've never been with anyone. Quentin's the only person I've ever had any interest in, even when it seemed like it might never be reciprocated.

"You can come back to our cabin to sleep if you want, Felix. To give them some privacy," Helena says.

Quentin surprises me by lifting his head and snarling. "No."

I blink at him, trying to turn when I hear footsteps coming closer to us. I can't see my sister or stupid Felix with the way I'm facing Quentin.

"Don't worry, Q. I'm not going anywhere. I'll be in my bedroom, alright?" Felix says softly, reaching over me to ruffle Quentin's hair.

My vision goes red, a snarl escaping me as I snap my teeth

at his hand. He pulls away quickly with a laugh, and Quentin smiles down at me in amusement. I glare at Quentin and say, "You're *mine*. He can't just come over here and touch you like that. Not ever, but especially not while I'm *right here.*"

"Sorry, *Luna*. Didn't realize you'd be so jealous." Felix snickers.

Quentin growls out a warning, and Felix mumbles an apology. I ignore him and snuggle closer to my mate, burying my face against his throat and breathing in his summery, sunshine scent until it's the only thing my brain can focus on. I vaguely hear Helena leave the cabin, and Felix's footsteps retreating as the lights are turned off.

"Get some sleep, Nico," Quentin whispers, kissing the top of my head.

Lying there in my mate's arms on a cramped, outdated couch in a dusty old cabin, I manage to drift off into the most peaceful sleep I've ever had.

FIVE

QUENTIN

Vanilla, cinnamon, and sugar. That incredible scent is the first thing I notice when I wake up. I smile and rub my nose against the top of Nico's head without opening my eyes, wrapping my arms around him tighter. He hums in his sleep and rubs his cheek against my chest while curling his fingers against my tee shirt. My smile grows wider, and I finally open my eyes to look down at him.

The mate bond is wild. Less than twenty-four hours ago, I dreaded finding my mate and was convinced a mate bond would be no better than living under the control of my dad. I was also certain I hated the twins. But now? Goddess, Nico and I have barely talked about being mates, and he's already the most precious thing in the world to me.

The sun's peeking through the blinds in the kitchen and living room windows, but my phone is on the coffee table where I can't reach it, so I have no idea what time it is. My guess is it's still pretty early though. I can hear Felix snoring in one of the bedrooms, and I don't hear any commotion outside. With as many wolves as there are on the property, this place is insanely noisy during the day.

Despite only getting a few hours of sleep, I've never felt

more at peace or well-rested. Everything feels like it's falling into place perfectly. Even my dad doesn't feel like as much of a threat. Now that I've got my mate, I'll do anything it takes to protect him and make him happy for the rest of my life. There's nothing my dad can do to stop that from happening.

"Quentin?" Nico asks in a quiet, sleepy voice, nuzzling his cheek against my chest.

"Yeah, sweetheart?" The pet name slips out my mouth, and my smile grows impossibly wider.

He tilts his head back and meets my eyes, smiling shyly as he grips my tee shirt tighter between his fingers. "So, um, you didn't change your mind?"

My eyebrows shoot up. I growl and turn onto my back, pulling him on top of me. I lose my mind for a second at the feel of his weight on me, sliding my hands down his back and onto his perfect, tight ass. I've never been attracted to a guy before, but damn. Nico looks and smells delicious, and after all the shit I googled and watched on Pornhub last night, I can't wait to explore *all the things* with him.

Shaking my head, I force myself to focus on the present. And the fact that my mate thinks I'll change my mind about him for some fucking reason. I frown at him and ask, "Why would you think that?"

He shrugs and drops his gaze, focusing on my chest. "I don't know. A lot of reasons, I guess? Last night, you ran off after saying you were straight just so you could hang out with your beta. Plus, I've had a crush on you forever, but it's like you never noticed or cared. You've always acted like you hated me."

Guilt eats away at me. I *did* hate Nico and his sister until yesterday, and I feel terrible for that. If we can just be honest with each other and get to know each other properly, I don't think there will be any problems between us going forward. The Moon Goddess brought us together, didn't she? We're supposed to be meant for each other. I feel bad that my mate feels insecure. I need to make him see that I'm committed to him one hundred percent, no question.

"I had no idea you had a crush on me." I smirk, lightly squeezing his ass. The tiny gasp that spills from his lips drives me wild, and I know I'm not mistaking the hint of arousal in his scent. I growl playfully and grind my hips against his, feeling his dick stir against mine through our sweatpants. "I'm sorry I was blind to you before yesterday, but I promise I'm definitely not anymore."

His cheeks flush scarlet, and he furrows his eyebrows angrily. Fucking adorable. "Ugh, no. You can't do that. You're trying to distract me by being all sexy and pretending like none of that stuff is a big deal."

Part of me is beyond pleased that he thinks anything about me is sexy, but I realize it's not the time to focus on that. I reach up to cup his cheek, gently tilting his head up until he settles his pretty caramel eyes on mine. I was hoping I could wait at least a little longer before telling him the truth about everything, but I don't see what other choice I have.

"Alright. I'm sorry. The truth is, I've spent pretty much my entire life focused on surviving and keeping Felix safe. My dad is...he's not a good guy, Nico. He's cruel when he thinks nobody's watching, and he's involved in a lot of bad, dangerous shit. Every time you and Helena came around, so hell bent on getting me into trouble or proving to my dad what a worthless alpha I am? He made me pay for that. Even worse, he made *Felix* pay for that. His favorite way to punish me has always been to order me to be still and silent while he beats my best friend in front of me."

What I don't tell Nico is that when I first met Felix, I thought I was saving him. His parents died when he was five, and he ended up living with his alpha at the time in a small, weak-ass pack in some middle-of-nowhere town in New Mexico. Officially, my dad brought me along with him to check in on his packs scattered throughout our territory. Unofficially, I'm pretty sure he was doing some shady business with that other alpha. While they were busy talking, I went exploring and sniffing around the property. I found Felix chained up in a shed on the edge of the pack's land. He was naked, starved, and had been hurt with silver so his injuries couldn't heal. I barely remember making the conscious decision to make him my beta after I got him free—I just did it. I thought binding him to me would force my dad to bring him back home with us. Which he did, even though he was pissed. I just didn't realize he'd end up using my friendship with Felix against me.

Felix swears that the abuse we've endured from my dad is nothing compared to how he was treated by his old alpha, but goddess, he deserves better. It took him a long time to tell me about all the things that happened to him in his old pack, and he still has nightmares sometimes. I'd never betray his trust by telling Nico about his past—that's Felix's decision, if he ever decides to tell anyone else. I just need my mate to realize that Felix and I are a package deal, and that he doesn't need to be jealous of the connection I share with my best friend.

Nico gapes at me, his eyes filling with tears. "Goddess. Quentin, I—I had no idea."

"I know you didn't, sweetheart." I brush my thumb over his cheek, smiling sadly. "Nobody knows what my dad is really like, and I'm not gonna hold anything *he* did against you. When I realized you were my mate last night, I was happy. Confused, sure, because I've only ever been attracted to females before. But mostly, I was happy. Until I thought about my dad. He's not going to be happy about us being mates, and I guarantee he's gonna try to find some way to ruin this. I panicked at the thought of not being able to protect you from him. That's why I freaked out and ran off. But Felix talked some sense into me. I'm never gonna let anything bad happen to you, Nico. I'm gonna spend the rest of my life learning everything about you, figuring out every single way to make you smile, and doing anything it takes to make you love me. Alright?"

"I—" he whimpers, a few tears falling from his eyes. Before I can wipe them away or sit up so I can do a better job of comforting him, he leans down and crashes his lips to mine.

It's rough and messy, and his teeth clack against mine. But I still can't help smiling like an idiot against his lips while I hug him tighter. It's the best kiss of my life. Goddess, he's fucking perfect.

"I'm sorry." He pulls away with a grimace, his face turning red and blotchy all the way down to his neck. "That was my first kiss."

Maybe I shouldn't be surprised, but I am. Most wolves—especially those of us from traditional packs—are told to save ourselves for our mate. The Kallises are pretty traditional and powerful, *and* Nico's admitted he's had a crush on me since he was a kid. I guess it's not that strange to realize I'll be his first *everything.* For the first time, I feel guilty about my own past sexual experiences. I've been with eight females—all random, human girls I met while traveling the world with Felix over the past year. They were all nice and pretty, but none of them really meant anything. Still, I don't want to risk making Nico jealous. But I don't want to lie to him either.

I decide not to say anything at all about my own experience. Not unless he asks. I give him a goofy smile and ruffle his hair. "Guess I should apologize for being so presumptuous with all of the stuff you read in my notebook, huh?"

He laughs, and I decide it's my new favorite sound in the entire world. "No. You don't have to apologize for that." His smile drops, and he lifts his hand to cup my cheek. "You don't have to apologize for anything. I feel terrible for making any assumptions about you and for judging you all these years. I was so embarrassingly obsessed with you from pretty much the first moment we met. Every time you ignored me or acted annoyed by something I said or did, I'd get so mad and hurt.

Helena and I assumed you were a spoiled brat who thought you were better than us because you're older and because of who your dad is. Helena was scared you'd end up being her mate and that you'd expect us to take over a pack in your dad's territory. She thought if she won enough challenges between you, you'd be forced to admit she's the stronger alpha so that *we'd* get to pick where we claim our territory."

Hearing everything from his perspective—how he saw me all these years and all the assumptions he made—brings a smile to my face. Maybe it's stupid, but it's just proof to me that we're gonna be alright. We're gonna be fucking perfect together.

"We can claim our territory wherever the fuck you want, sweetheart." I lift my head to capture his lips in a quick kiss, pulling back with a grin. "The further away from Texas, the better, in my opinion." Something else occurs to me. The twins are only seventeen. "You've still got another year of high school left, right?"

He shakes his head. "We graduated a year early. Lena and I are supposed to be starting at Red Cedar University in Washington this fall."

Over 1500 miles away from my dad's territory? That's perfect. Giving Nico a sly, flirtatious grin, I growl and flip us so that I'm on top of him. He gasps quietly, and I lean down to whisper in his ear. "Graduated early, huh? Always knew you were a smarty-pants. I think I owe you congratulations. And an apology for missing your graduation ceremony."

I nibble lightly on his ear, and he whines low in his throat as he bucks his hips against mine. I'm fully hard, and I'm beyond pleased to realize he is too.

"You missed my birthday too," he says, practically panting as he tilts his head sideways to expose his throat. "Two of them. I was so mad at you for leaving *right* before my sixteenth birthday when I got my mate mark. And then I had to follow stupid Felix on Instagram to see what you were up to all year because you don't have any social media accounts of your own."

"Poor baby." I chuckle, sliding my tongue from his ear to his throat. I bite down gently, eliciting a moan from him. Fuck. I was wrong earlier. *This* is my new favorite sound in the world. "How am I ever gonna make it up to you?"

"Glad to see you two getting along."

I look up to find Felix standing in the hallway, grinning smugly at us with his arms crossed. I must have been too focused on Nico to hear him get up, but I'm happy to see he looks well-rested. I chuckle and flip him off, and then I look back down at Nico as I wiggle my eyebrows. "I think we're more than *getting along.*"

Nico chokes, smacking my chest while he shoots a glare at Felix. His face is so red, it's fucking adorable. I can't tell if he's mad at Felix for interrupting us, or if he's embarrassed at having an audience. Either way, I mentally add 'making Nico blush' to the top of my list of new favorite things.

Felix snickers and walks into the kitchen, pulling a Dr. Pepper out of the fridge. As he cracks it open, he raises his eyebrows at me. "What's our plan for the day?"

I know what he's really asking. What's the plan for dealing with my dad? I still have no fucking idea. Just thinking about it makes me anxious. But I meant what I said to Nico. I'm not gonna let my dad ruin this. There's no way I'll be able to avoid him all day. I'll be lucky if I can get a few hours before he tracks me down and learns about me and Nico. I haven't asked him about *his* parents either. Are they going to react badly? How difficult is it gonna be for us to get out of here without any drama or bloodshed?

"Is our shit still packed?" I ask Felix.

He nods. "Mostly. It'll only take me a couple minutes to get everything together."

Good. That'll make it easier in case we need to make a quick getaway. I hope Nico and Helena have all their shit still mostly packed too. If we can load our cars up now, I'll feel more comfortable about having to confront our parents.

Nico stares up at me with wide eyes, worrying his bottom lip between his teeth. I want him to know the truth about my dad so he can be careful and cautious, but I don't want him to be scared. I lean down and give him a soft kiss, pulling away with a goofy smile. "You wanna go get some breakfast? There's this diner about twenty minutes off-property where they make the best fucking pancakes in the universe."

SIX

NICO

I try to glare at Helena, but I'm smiling way too big to make it convincing. Quentin hasn't stopped touching me or doting on me since we woke up, and I feel like I'm on cloud nine. I have to keep pinching myself to make sure I'm not dreaming every time I turn to find him looking at me like I'm his whole world.

My twin smirks and winks at me. I give up trying to look mad, looking back down to focus on the way that Quentin is carefully cutting up my pancakes. His eyebrows are furrowed like he's concentrating on a difficult task. It's so unnecessary, but way too adorable to ask him to stop. I'm a high-ranking wolf with my beta status, and I'm almost as strong as Helena. Honestly, I could probably hold my own in a fight against most alphas, Quentin included. I never thought I would enjoy being babied and completely fawned over by my mate.

But seeing Quentin act like this? So sweet and attentive like I'm something delicate and precious? I love it. I'm surprised I haven't melted into a puddle from the way he's been treating me.

It's also incredibly jarring seeing him this way. In the past, he was always really indifferent about pretty much everything whenever me and Helena were around. And if not indifferent, then he was pissed off or annoyed at us. Guilt burns in my chest, just thinking about it. I know why he was like that now. I was crushing on him so hard for *years*, and it never occurred to me that he was keeping his true feelings or emotions hidden for some reason. I also never realized how much my sister and I were inadvertently hurting him with our actions and behavior. It's no wonder he never showed any real interest in me before. Goddess, I'm lucky he's willing to accept me as his mate at all after everything.

"Aww, come on." Felix laughs, shoving a forkful of French toast into his mouth. I wrinkle my nose when he continues talking with his mouth full. "I guarantee you'll be the same way when you meet your own Luna."

Helena rolls her eyes, and I snort as I shake my head at him. "You do know that *Luna* is supposed to be used for female alphas who are mated to male alphas, right?"

Felix grins at me, his eyes lighting up mischievously. "My bad. I didn't realize we were the sort of pack to follow such strict rules."

My lips curve into a smile. He has a point. I don't know any werewolves who are mated to someone the same sex they are. I've never even heard of it happening. Most packs don't have two alphas who aren't mated to each other either, like our pack has with Helena and Quentin. There's really nothing traditional about us anymore.

"I just hope my mate isn't an asshole." Helena sighs, resting her elbows on the table across from me. "And it's definitely asking a lot, but I hope they're not an alpha."

She's such a control freak, I know it would drive her crazy to have a mate who's anywhere near as bossy as she is. Even though Quentin's an alpha too, he doesn't seem that interested in leading our pack. Since we left the pack-gathering to go get breakfast—together as a pack for the first time—we've been talking and catching up. It's been nice, being able to be so free and casual around Quentin. And I guess…Felix really isn't so bad. Now that I know he and Quentin never had a thing.

Felix bumps his elbow against Helena's, that charming grin lighting up his face again. "Trust me. You'll be just as infatuated and sappy as Q over there no matter who your mate ends up being."

Quentin shoots me a way-too-sexy smile, dousing my pancakes in maple syrup. He slides my plate in front of me, leaning close to give me a surprise peck on the lips. My cheeks warm up, and my heart flips over a million times in my chest. For a guy who thought he was straight less than twenty-four hours ago, he's sure not embarrassed or hesitant about being affectionate with me in public. Goddess, I love it so much.

"Like you won't be the same way," Helena grumbles at Felix, baring her teeth angrily when he grins smugly.

I want to kick her under the table to warn her to chill out, but I know that would only make a scene. I haven't had a real chance to talk to her yet. Not about any of the things Quentin told me this morning when we woke up. She still has no idea how awful Quentin's dad is, or that he hurts Felix to punish Quentin. I told her I want us to go back to Houston today, and she didn't question me. She just helped load all of our stuff back up in our car before we came to the diner.

"I won't," Felix says with a smirk. He holds his wrist up for us to see. "I'm mateless. So, no. No mate for me."

"What?" Helena and I say at the same time, gaping at Felix's bare wrist. Helena reaches out to pull his arm closer to her, leaning over the table to inspect it carefully as if his mark is hiding where we can't easily see.

"It's no big deal." Felix laughs. But it doesn't sound like his usual laugh, and I swear I see a flash of pain in his eyes.

I've never met anyone mateless before. How have we known Felix for so long without realizing it? It's so rare. Even rarer than a wolf having a human as their mate. Before my sixteenth birthday, I used to worry I'd end up mateless. My parents and Helena always reassured me I wouldn't be—that it's usually only omegas that happens to—but their reassurances never put me at ease. I've known I'm gay basically my whole life, and it seemed more likely at the time that I'd end up mateless than with another male as my mate.

Leaning against Quentin, I let out a sigh of relief and send a silent thank you to the Moon Goddess for pairing us together. Now I'll never have to worry again.

Poor Felix though. I really haven't given him a fair chance, have I? I've hated him for years, all because I thought Quentin liked him or that they had a secret relationship. After the way I've treated him, he should hate me too, but he's been nothing but nice and supportive since he found out that Quentin and I are mates.

"Just because you don't have a mark, that doesn't mean you don't have a soulmate out there somewhere," Quentin says. He reaches across the table to pat Felix's arm. My eye twitches, and I purse my lips to hold in a growl. I *know* they don't have romantic feelings for each other—and I'm quickly learning that they're both very affectionate in general—but I still don't like my mate touching someone else. Quentin grins at his beta, oblivious to my jealousy, and adds, "Just means it might be harder to find them. I bet you'll end up with a pretty little human."

Goddess, my mate is so sweet. I've always known he was fun, cool, strong, adventurous, and insanely hot. But I had no idea he was so fucking *sweet*. He's not even talking to me, but his words to his beta make me want to tackle him right here in the booth and kiss the absolute crap out of him.

"Thanks, Q." Felix smiles, his smile appearing much more genuine as his shoulders relax.

"Speaking of mates..." Quentin turns to me with this smile that makes me flush from head to toe. Does he even realize how sexy he is? He leans close enough to playfully nip my ear and growls softly, instantly making me hard. When he pulls away just enough to meet my eyes, he says in a husky voice, "The full moon's only a few days away."

My eyes widen, and I choke on my spit. I haven't taken a bite of my pancakes yet, so I can't use them as an excuse. It's just...I can't believe he's bringing up the full moon so quickly after realizing we're mates. I can't believe he's bringing it up in front of Helena and Felix!

"I—" This embarrassing wheezy laugh escapes me, and I struggle to form any more words as I stare up into Quentin's pretty green eyes. I feel like I'm daydreaming again. To solidify our mate bond, we have to mark each other during a full moon. I haven't let myself hope that Quentin would want to complete the bond so soon. I've barely let myself accept the idea that he wants me, period.

"Sorry," Quentin whispers, his eyes filling with worry. He swipes a hand through his already-messy hair and gives me a nervous smile. "I didn't mean to put you on the spot. I'd mark you right now if I could, but I understand if you wanna wait."

Wait? Absolutely not. To be honest, I'm about a second away from blurting out that I love him and that I'd let him mark me and fuck me right here and now if I could. Three days feels like too long to wait. My hesitation is only because of my insecurities that he'll change his mind. I worry that he'll realize he can do better, or that he'll decide he still finds me just as annoying as he did before he knew I was his mate.

Most wolves complete their mating bonds right away. It's why so many pack-gatherings like this one usually take place so close to the full moon. I'm worried and nervous that I'm gonna do something to screw this up. I still feel like a stupid kid obsessing over Quentin, following him around and hoping he'll notice me. I'm terrified to show him just how eager I am to be his.

"Maybe you should take him on a date first, Q?" Felix says, sounding amused. "Remember how we talked about wooing your mate last night?"

Quentin's face lights up with a smile, and he never once looks away from me. "Yeah, that's a good idea. You wanna go on a date, Nico? Let me take you out to dinner tonight after we get settled back at your place. Where's your favorite place in Houston? We should go there too."

"Take him to the Museum of Natural Science, and you'll win all the brownie points," Helena says teasingly.

Before I have time to feel embarrassed that my twin is outing me for being such a geek, Quentin leans forward to kiss my cheek and says, "Noted."

The rest of breakfast is nice. More than nice. There's no awkwardness, no tension, and it's a really sweet peek at what life could be like for the four of us as a pack. The pancakes Quentin suggested I order are hands down the tastiest I've ever had, just like he promised they'd be, and he never stops touching me the entire time we're eating and sitting together at the booth. He keeps his leg pressed against mine, his arm around my waist, and he frequently leans over to sniff me, nuzzle me, or surprise me with soft kisses.

While I'm busy swooning, blushing, and thanking the Moon Goddess for the millionth time, Quentin, Felix, and Helena talk like we've all been the best of friends for years. Helena mentions our original summer plans—to basically chill by the pool at our house in Houston for the next two months before driving up to Washington to settle into our new home and territory in time for us to start school. The guys seem more than happy to tag along, and we agree that the summer will give us plenty of time to bond properly as a new pack.

I'm riveted while Quentin and Felix tell us about all the places they've traveled over the past year. I've been obsessively tracking them the best I can since they graduated, but all I've had to go on before now were sporadic Instagram posts from Felix. I'd love to travel like that someday. Not just to fancy, touristy resorts like my family stays in whenever we go on vacation. I want a *real* adventure like Quentin and his beta. Trekking through dense jungles, running along remote and secluded beaches in our wolf forms, and climbing the tallest mountains all over the world.

Hearing details about the life Quentin's been living over the past year makes me excited, but it also makes me jealous and anxious. Will he be satisfied with me? Being stuck in a small college town in Washington for the next few years while I finish my degree? I have no idea if he has plans for college. All I know is that he wants to get away from his dad's territory.

"Will you guys be going to uni with us when we move to Washington?" Helena asks, as if she can read my mind.

Felix and Quentin share a look, and Quentin shrugs at him. "You should, at least. I bet we can get your deferred acceptance to UNM switched over to Red Cedar University fairly easily." He surprises me by turning to me, giving me a sweet and shy smile. "I don't know what I'm going to do yet. Probably not college—I'm not smart like you guys are. But I'll get a job and figure it out. Find a way to make you proud to be my mate."

"I'm already proud," I say. And even though I'm nervous and inexperienced, I force myself to be brave and give him a kiss. If he's not worried about an audience, then I shouldn't worry either. He smiles against my lips, wrapping his arms around my waist to pull me closer. When I pull away from the kiss, butterflies fluttering like mad in my stomach, I smile at him and add, "And I don't want to wait to complete our bond either. I'm glad the full moon is so soon."

Pride, joy, and lust dance in his eyes, and he pulls me into his lap so that I'm straddling him. I let out a short, surprised laugh, but it's quickly cut off when Quentin crashes his lips against mine.

"Goddess!" Helena hisses at us while Felix snickers beside her. She growls, using her alpha voice to reprimand us. "We're in public, idiots!"

I couldn't care less, and it's pretty obvious Quentin feels the same way.

QUENTIN

"ARE YOU OKAY?" NICO ASKS QUIETLY.

Felix turns in his seat to frown at me, and Helena meets my eyes in the rearview mirror. I'm glad she's driving so that I can focus on Nico and try to distract myself from the fact that we're heading back to the pack-gathering. We spent over three hours at the diner. I guarantee my dad's looking for me by now. Felix and I turned our phones off when we left our cabin this morning, and my dad's probably already called and texted me a dozen times.

He's always furious with me when we go dark like this. He gave me some leniency while I was traveling with Felix, but only because a lot of the places we went didn't have cell service. Even then, the few times we went too long being unreachable, he threatened to send some of his top wolves to hunt us down and drag us home. There's no doubt in my mind that he'd do something that insane, and then punish me and Felix for it severely later. It's why I've never tried to run away in an official capacity, to break away from him and his territory. I've always worried he'd be able to find me no matter where I went, and the repercussions would be worse than anything I've experienced under his control before.

"You remember what I told you about my dad?" I ask Nico. I don't want to worry him, but I need to prepare him as much as I can. He nods slowly, his eyes filling with sympathy. I take a shaky breath and rub my hand over Nico's back affectionately. "He's probably looking for me by now, which means I'm gonna have to face him as soon as we get back. I'm worried about what he's gonna say or do when he finds out you're my mate."

Helena makes an angry sound in the back of her throat, meeting my eyes in the rearview mirror again. "You think he'll be angry? It's not like we have any control over the Moon Goddess or who she chooses as our mates."

Obviously, I agree with her, but my dad doesn't think rationally. The only thing he'll be worried about is appearances. He's the strongest alpha in the country, and he wants people to think he's an example of what all wolves should aspire to. My older sisters are mated to strong alphas who helped expand the territory, and my sisters have both done nothing over the past several years except pop out a bunch of kids just like they were always expected to. My dad has expectations for me too. He expects me to find my mate—a *female* who I can have a bunch of pups with—and settle into a pack that'll make his territory stronger. I'm sure he expects me to help him with some of his illegal endeavors too—I know my sister's mates are involved—but I've worked hard to act ignorant to a lot of things over the years.

When he finds out that Nico's my mate, I just *know* he's going to be furious. Because I won't be able to get Nico pregnant and biologically have a bunch of pups to carry on the fucking Peterson legacy. I'm sure he'll be equally pissed that Nico's not an alpha. My dad already hates the fact that I chose a supposed omega to be my beta—and a mateless one at that.

"What about your parents?" I ask Helena and Nico. "They're pretty traditional too, aren't they?"

Helena shrugs, and Nico gives me a sad smile. "Kind of.

They know I'm gay though, so I know they won't be mad I have you as my mate. I think they might be disappointed you're not Lena's mate is all. They've always wanted you two to be together since you're both strong alphas, and I'm sure they were hoping you guys would combine our territories. Plus, they think you guys will have cute babies."

Nico's eyebrows scrunch together, and there's an adorable, jealous pout on his face. I pull him to my side and kiss the top of his head. "Well, I'm really fucking glad *you're* my mate, and I don't care what anyone thinks. I just wanna make sure your parents aren't gonna try to force us apart or some shit."

"Will your dad try to force us apart?" Nico gasps, his eyes widening in fear.

It kills me to admit it, to scare or worry him, but I have to be truthful. I nod slowly, pulling him closer when he lets out a quiet whimper. I growl and look over at my new co-alpha. "Helena, promise me that whatever my dad tries to do, protect Nico and Felix. Get them in the car and take off if things get bad, alright?"

She meets my eyes with a steely expression and nods once. My shoulders relax slightly. I'm glad we're on the same page. I know I can trust her to take care of them. The rest of the drive back to the gathering is tense and silent. I hold Nico close, rubbing his back and nuzzling his hair to comfort him the best I can. When I see Felix trembling slightly in the passenger seat, my heart clenches. Before I can ask him to come sit in the back with me and Nico so I can comfort him too, Helena reaches over and pats his head before threading her fingers through his. I can't help smiling. We've only been a pack for a couple of hours, but it's already obvious we're going to work well together. I can't wait to get away and start fresh. To claim our own territory far away from my dad's toxic bullshit.

When we reach the gates outside the property of the gathering, I turn my phone on. Just like I expected, I have several missed calls and texts from my dad. Each message from him is angrier and more demanding than the last. His alpha order doesn't work the same over text as it does when I can physically hear his voice, but I still feel myself flinch at the words on the screen.

"I won't let him hurt you." Nico growls, leaning over me to read the texts.

That's the least of my concerns—all I'm worried about is keeping Nico and Felix safe and as far from my dad as I can. But knowing my mate feels protective over me too makes my heart flip. It makes me feel more confident and prepared to face my father's wrath. Once I confront him and let him know that Nico's my mate, I have every intention of getting the fuck out of his territory. Hopefully forever. He won't be able to order me to do shit once I complete my bond with Nico.

Wolves run freely and happily around the property. A few yip at the car in excitement as we drive down the path to the main building. I smile sadly at the sight. While I hate my dad and I feel imprisoned in his territory, most of the wolves and packs he leads are decent. They're just regular people living their lives. Minus a few select alphas, most of the wolves who live in the territory are ignorant to my dad's true demeanor and illegal activities.

"Oh, crap." Helena sighs heavily. My arms tense around Nico, but before I can ask what's wrong, I see what's caught her attention. Her and Nico's parents are standing outside the doors of the main building, talking to my dad.

I get a sour taste in my mouth. Nico made it sound like his parents won't care too much about us being mates, but I can't help thinking the worst. They look so content while they share pleasantries with my dad.

My eyes meet my dad's as we pass, irritation marring his expression. I take a deep breath and give Nico a quick kiss before opening the door and helping him out. Glancing over my shoulder, I see Nico's parents waving at us from their spot in front of the main building. A few other wolves—in human and wolf form—mill around, stopping to offer greetings as they pass. A few feet away from the Kallises, my dad stands with his arms crossed in front of him. To everyone else, I'm sure he appears stoic and slightly intimidating. But I can practically feel the anger rolling off of him as he waits for me to approach him.

There is some relief, knowing we have an audience. He's less likely to cause a huge scene when the Kallises and so many other wolves are around. That doesn't mean he'll be nice or make shit easy. But I know in my soul he'd behave much worse if we were to confront him in private.

"Ready, sweetheart?" I wrap my arm around Nico's waist, pulling him close to my side. He smiles up at me and nods, his dark curls falling into his soft brown eyes. After checking to make sure Felix and Helena are following, I pull Nico along with me over to my dad.

I keep my head held high and a slightly cocky smile on my face. No matter how nervous I am, I refuse to show any weakness. It's not as hard to fake my confidence as usual. Despite my initial surprise, I'm proud to have Nico on my arm. He's a fucking catch—he's hot, he's smart, and he's a strong wolf from an influential family. Focusing on the future we can have together and how much fun it's going to be getting to know him for real gives me so much motivation to get through this moment. With everything I have to look forward to, I know I'll be able to get through this.

"We were wondering where you were," Nico's mom says when we approach. She smiles at the twins, her gaze falling on my arm around Nico's waist.

Her eyebrows shoot up curiously. Before she can voice her question, my dad growls to capture my attention. When I turn to meet his steely blue eyes, he frowns and says, "Yes, I would love to hear an explanation for why your phone was off. I've been trying to reach you all morning."

It's not a question, but the authority in his alpha voice is indisputable. My wolf bristles under my skin, giving me enough courage to rebel against my dad's usual bullshit. I give him a wide, slightly unhinged smile and lean down to kiss Nico's cheek as I rub my hand over his hip.

"I turned my phone off so I could enjoy breakfast with my mate," I say with a carefree laugh. When Nico stares up at me like he can't decide if he's amused or if he thinks I'm insane, I feel my expression soften.

Nico's mom gasps, and I look up to find her staring at us with her hands over her mouth. The twins' dad stands at her side, gaping at us with a comical expression. My anxiety ratchets up at their reactions. I really hope they're more accepting than my dad and that they don't make Nico feel badly for being my mate. He deserves nothing but love, happiness, and acceptance from everyone important in his life.

"Oh, my goodness! Really?" his mom squeals. She steps forward, her eyes dropping excitedly to our wrists. Nico and I laugh, holding our hands out side by side to show off our matching marks.

"We ran into each other last night and realized," Nico says softly, a slight tremble in his voice. He hugs me tighter and laughs nervously. "Are you disappointed, mom?"

She looks offended by the question, shaking her head quickly. "Of course not! Oh, sweetie, I'm so thrilled you've found your mate! And we've always liked Quentin. He's such a good boy." She grins at me and cups my cheek in a motherly way before frowning in concern at her son. "Are you happy?"

"Goddess, yes. I'm ecstatic!" Nico laughs, looking up at me with a lovestruck expression that makes my heart beat faster.

His mom squeals again, pulling us into a hug. I'm sure I'm smiling like an idiot when I hug her back, but I'm so relieved that she's taking this well. When she pulls away, Nico's dad steps forward with a proud smile and reaches out to shake my hand.

"Congratulations," Alpha Kallis says excitedly. "It's a pleasure to welcome you to our family."

"Thank you both so much," I say to Nico's parents.

I feel relieved tears prick at the corners of my eyes, but I quickly blink them away. There will be time to reflect and focus on my emotions later. Remembering my dad's presence, I turn to gauge his reaction. His face is bright red, his lips are pursed, and there's a vein bulging on his forehead.

He seems to snap out of his stupor when I meet his eyes, and he snarls as he uses his alpha voice. "No. This has to be a mistake. The Moon Goddess would never do this to *my* son."

My entire body tenses, and I growl under my breath as I pull Nico closer to my side. A quick glance over my shoulder reassures me that Helena is standing protectively with Felix a safe distance away from my dad.

"Times are changing, Peterson." Alpha Kallis laughs casually, but it's easy to see that he's annoyed. "I'm sure you heard about that alpha up in Colorado. Three pups from his pack share a mate. We have no control over what the Moon Goddess does, but this is hardly such a dramatic or unfortunate situation. Haven't we always hoped our children would be mated?"

Three wolves sharing one mate!? The idea is both intriguing and appalling. Just thinking of Nico being with anyone other than me makes me feel violent and possessive. Still, I agree with Alpha Kallis's sentiment. Who are we to question the Moon Goddess? Having a mate is a gift—one I intend to treasure for the rest of my life.

"The fucking *Moon Goddess* is clearly punishing us." My dad snarls, stomping over to stand in front of me. He roughly grabs my wrist and holds it up to inspect my mate mark, digging his nails into my skin. I grit my teeth to keep myself from flinching, holding perfectly still when he continues growling furiously. "I should have known you'd have a defective mark. You chose a defective beta, and you've always been such a disappointment. You're barely a fucking alpha."

My eye twitches at the slight toward Felix, but I keep my mouth shut. He can say whatever he wants about me. I don't give a shit what he thinks. All I care about is finding a way *out*, far away from him and his control.

When he reaches for Nico's wrist, that's when I snap. I grab my dad's arm to stop him, a dangerous snarl rumbling in my throat as I push my mate behind me. I bare my teeth and meet my dad's eyes, standing taller so we're nearly the same height.

"Don't touch him. You'll never fucking touch him."

He trembles furiously, that vein on his forehead making him appear like he's about to explode. Using his alpha voice, he demands, "Reject the bond, Quentin."

Nausea rolls through me, and I feel myself sway on my feet. Nico gasps quietly and grips me tighter, but all I can focus on is the pain from my dad's order. My wolf fights desperately against it, and I bite the inside of my cheek so hard that I taste blood. Is it even possible for him to force me to break such a sacred bond?

Thank the Goddess, it seems it's not. My mate bond with Nico is stronger than any alpha order. The realization makes me grin, and I shove my dad back roughly to get him the fuck away from my mate.

"No. He's my mate, and during the full moon, I'm gonna mark him, fuck him, and make him mine forever."

I hear Helena and Felix snort behind me, but I don't have the chance to address them. Hearing them reminds me that we're in public. I quickly glance around, seeing several wolves standing nearby to eavesdrop on the situation. Good. If this makes my dad look like a shitty person, I'm glad for it.

My dad seems to remember that we have an audience at the same time I do. His expression shutters, and he leans close to me as he whispers in a dangerously low voice. "If you don't reject this disgusting excuse for a bond, I will cut you off financially. You'll lose your trust fund, you'll be banned from my territory, and I'll no longer consider you my son."

I vaguely hear the outraged protests from Nico's parents and some other wolves in the background, but they're not important. What *is* important is that my dad is somehow unbelievably offering me my freedom on a silver platter.

"Promise?" I ask with a psychotic grin.

He snarls, pulling his fist back and hitting me with a powerful right hook. Stupidly caught by surprise, I reel back and yelp in pain. My dad purposely wears silver rings for this exact reason—to make sure Felix and I will feel it when he hits us, and so it'll take days to heal instead of minutes.

Nico shifts into his wolf beside me, lunging toward my dad with a snarl. I manage to grab him just in time, wrapping my arms around his body and cradling him close to my chest. He wiggles and growls in protest, but I swore I wouldn't let my dad touch him. It's cute that he's trying to protect and defend me, but I'm not going to give my dad the chance to hurt my mate.

"He's not worth it, sweetheart." I run my fingers through Nico's thick, black fur. It's been a long time since I've seen him in his wolf form. He's bigger than I remember, which is to be expected. When I spot the white tip on his tail—the only spot of color on his black coat—I smile. Goddess, everything about him is adorable.

Turning my back on my dad, I grin at Felix and Helena as I carry Nico to our cars. There's no reason for us to stick around, as far as I'm concerned. Helena says something to her parents, who still seem furious and completely outraged by my dad's reaction to me and Nico. My dad screams at me as I retreat, threatening to snap my neck if I ever step foot in his territory again. He promises the same punishment to anyone in my pack, including Felix and Nico.

But I couldn't care less. Anything I'm losing today—

money I don't give a shit about, and a half-assed relationship with my mom and sisters who usually forget I exist—it all means nothing compared to what I'm gaining.

Nico shifts back into his human form when I reach the rental car Felix and I drove here in. I set him down, still holding him close, and he pouts up at me.

"You should have let me bite him," he whines. He raises his hand and trails his fingertips over my cheek. I wince at the sting—there's no doubt I'll have a black eye for a couple days, but I don't mind. I've had worse.

"So vicious, Luna," Felix teases, walking up behind Nico. There's a glimmer of concern in his eyes as he checks me over, and I grin to let him know that I'm good.

When Helena joins us, I feel my wolf relax and I breathe a sigh of relief. We just need to get off the property, and then we'll be safe. Hopefully for good. I wish we could all ride in the same vehicle to make it easier to keep an eye on the whole pack, but I have to return the rental first. Nico already agreed to ride with me while Felix rides in Helena's Land Rover. After we drop the rental off, the four of us will be able to stick together all the way back to the twins' home in Houston. And hopefully we'll stick together every day from here on out, no matter where we end up.

"Let's get the fuck out of here." I grin at my pack.

EIGHT

QUENTIN

THE FULL MOON RISES ABOVE THE TREE LINE, AND I THROW MY head back to let out a loud, excited howl. Felix immediately calls back to me. I can't help wagging my tail when I hear how happy and carefree he sounds.

Nico growls and nips at my heels. If I could laugh in this form, I would. It's been a few days since we left the pack-gathering, and Nico is still jealous any time I so much as smile at my best friend. I've told him a million times that I've never once been interested in Felix like that—and most of the time, Felix and Nico seem to get along—but Nico can't help bristling whenever he feels like Felix and I are acting too friendly. Felix thinks it's hilarious, and I have to agree. The fact that my mate is so possessive of me brings my wolf an insane amount of pleasure, and he always looks so fucking adorable when he's angry or jealous.

When Nico nips my heel again, I growl playfully and turn to tackle him. He puts up a bit of a fight, but I'm a lot bigger than him in wolf form. He only submits when I bite his neck. The second he goes still, I wag my tail and lie flat on top of him, nuzzling his neck and the side of his head.

He snorts at me and thumps his tail, and I shift back into

my human form to grin down at him. I thread my fingers through his thick black fur and chuckle. "Don't tell me you're gonna spend the whole night being a brat."

After playfully nipping at my fingers, he shifts into his human form beneath me and pouts. "Shut up. I wasn't being a brat."

"Oh, really?" I cup his cheek and brush my thumb over his bottom lip. His tongue darts out to flick against my finger, and a quiet groan escapes me. He looks so fucking good under the moonlight like this. Can't wait to claim him as mine forever. Shaking my head, I focus on the conversation instead of how deliciously distracting he is. "So, you weren't getting pissy because Felix howled at me, huh? He's like a mile away, sweetheart."

Nico's mouth curves into a guilty smile, and he shrugs as he rubs his hands up and down my chest. "Is it really so wrong to want all of your attention on me tonight? It's our first full moon together."

I give him a seductive smile and lean down, hovering above him so our lips barely brush. He gasps quietly when I grind my hips against his, and I let out another pleased growl when I feel that he's already as hard as I am.

"You know you've got my attention," I say in a deep, raspy voice. Fuck, I've never been so turned on. All of my instincts are begging me to bite him, mark him, fuck him. Right now. If I don't solidify our bond, I feel like I might die. But the logical part of my brain fights against those feelings. I want everything to be perfect and special for my mate. "I've got a surprise for you."

He groans and wraps his legs around my waist, pulling me flush against him as he captures my lips in a searing kiss. "Please tell me the surprise is your dick in my mouth. I need you so fucking badly, Quentin."

My brain temporarily combusts and my fingers itch to rip his clothes off and turn him over onto his stomach. Tonight won't be our first time. We've been fucking damn near constantly since we left the pack gathering a few days ago. At least, anytime I'm not working. Nico's dad got me a job bussing tables and washing dishes at a restaurant his beta owns. It's nothing fancy, but it'll be nice to save up a little money before we move to Washington in a couple months. I've also been trying to woo Nico properly, but our dates don't seem to get very far before he practically jumps me and begs me to fuck him. Trying *all the things* has been a million times better than I anticipated.

But tonight *is* supposed to be special. We agreed we wanted to complete our bond the first chance we got, so I made plans. I spent hours putting his surprise together, and here he is—being a brat and testing my resolve.

"That is *not* the surprise." I laugh. It's extremely difficult, but I force myself to pull away. I give him one last teasing smile and tell him to follow me before shifting back into my wolf.

He groans, but I don't wait before taking off running. Nico's fast. Maybe faster than I am, so I know he'll catch up quick. Seconds later, I hear him run up behind me. I yip happily and push myself to run faster. I hear him snort in response and feel him nip my heel before moving to run shoulder-to-shoulder with me.

The property the Kallises own specifically to run on during full moons is made up of several hundred acres, and it's about an hour outside of Houston. It's a smaller area than I'm used to spending my full moons, but at least there are woods here. It's not just open desert like the properties my dad owns in New Mexico and West Texas. It's been weird, being here the past few days. Like we're stuck in some kind of limbo. We're not *that* far from my dad's territory, and the Kallises have been busy prepping and telling the rest of their wolves in their pack to be cautious along the border between them. It feels like I'm constantly waiting for something bad to happen.

Like things have been too perfect and have worked too well in my favor ever since I reunited with Nico.

But surprisingly, my dad hasn't tried to contact me at all. I thought it might have been too good to be true when he banished me and cut me off. I've been low-key worried he'd change his mind and track me down to punish me. After tonight, after I mark Nico and make him mine for eternity, my dad will never be able to control me again.

When I reach the far corner of the property—a place I made sure to check no other wolves would accidentally stumble across tonight—I bark at Nico and come to a stop. He turns and tilts his head at me curiously.

We're so different. Not only our wolf forms—his midnight black fur is distinct against my light gray coat—but our personalities too. He's so competitive, smart, organized, and detail-oriented about everything. I may have spent most of my life thinking he was annoying, but he acts exasperated with everything I say or do half the time too. He gets so worked up about the smallest things when I'd usually rather let things go or just go with the flow. Seeing him get so easily ruffled is one of my new favorite things. So is discovering all of his quirks, his likes and dislikes, and every interest or hobby he nerds out over.

Honestly, I love how different we are. It's going to make our life together way more interesting.

"Is this where my surprise is?" Nico asks after he shifts. He peers around curiously, brushing his curly hair away from his eyes.

I walk over to him and rub my muzzle against his leg before shifting behind him. Pulling him back against my chest, I wrap my arms around him and lean down to kiss his cheek. "Uh huh. Are you gonna be good so I can give it to you?"

He shivers and rubs his ass against me, making my dick twitch. "Depends. Does the surprise involve your giant cock in my ass?"

A choked laugh gets stuck in my throat, and I spin him around to kiss him. His tongue tangles with mine, and his hands move down my chest to unbutton my shorts. I force myself to pull away and grin down at him. "Can't you just *try* to let me be romantic for one night?"

"You're just so hot," he says shyly, giving me a guilty smile. "It's harder than usual tonight, with the full moon. Goddess, my wolf is begging me to mark you and let you dominate me. It's making me feel crazy, Quentin."

Hearing my mate tell me how desirable he finds me and how ready he is for me to mark him gives me so much fucking satisfaction. I cup Nico's face between my hands, tilting his head back so I can drink in his gorgeous features beneath the moonlight. I can't get over how stunning he is. Sometimes I feel like such an idiot for never really *seeing* him before. All the years we've known each other, and I doubt I would have ever looked at him twice if he wasn't my mate. I would have been too stuck on the idea that I was straight, and I'd probably still hold a grudge against him for all the ways he pissed me off when we were growing up.

But the Moon Goddess knew what she was doing, putting us together. Nico's perfect, and I'm gonna spend the rest of our lives making sure he knows how happy I am to be with him.

I'm filled with nervous anticipation as I kiss him softly and take his hand to lead him through the densest part of the woods. Nico's silent beside me—until he sees the first lantern and squeezes my fingers. I grin and pull him into the small clearing I set up for us tonight. There are about a dozen lanterns hanging from the trees, creating a wide circle around a cozy tent. The lighting from the lanterns and the moonlight gives the space a warm, romantic glow. Looking around, I'm pretty fucking proud of myself. It looks a million times nicer in this lighting than it did this afternoon.

"What's this?" Nico asks quietly.

I laugh and pull him closer to the tent. "You didn't really think I was gonna bend you over in the dirt to mark you with Felix, Helena, and your parents' pack running around less than a mile away from us, did you?"

Bending down to unzip the tent, I gently pull him inside so he can see how I've got it set up. I put another lantern in here—our eyesight is good in the dark, being werewolves, but the extra lighting definitely helps with the ambiance. There are about twenty blankets cushioning the floor of the tent, and close to a dozen pillows. I wanted to make it as comfortable for him as possible.

"When did you set this all up?" he asks in a quiet, awestruck voice.

"This afternoon," I say, rubbing my hand over his back. It's hard to tell what he's thinking. I think he likes it, but maybe I went a little overboard. Maybe he thinks I'm being ridiculous for wanting to make tonight special. Feeling more nervous with every passing second, I laugh and grab the cooler crammed in the corner. "I got some champagne too, and some strawberries. I know it's cheesy and cliché, but…"

Nico swallows audibly and turns to look at me, his caramel eyes practically sparkling in this light. "Being with you is nothing like I expected it would be. Even in my wildest fantasies, for as long as I spent crushing on you, I assumed you'd be…aloof. That you wouldn't really care about dating me or making romantic gestures. I thought it would be mostly physical for you, and I'd still be lucky to have that. But I was so wrong. Goddess, you're perfect. I constantly pinch myself to convince myself this is real. You're the best mate anyone could ever ask for, and I don't deserve you. This—this is so sweet and thoughtful. I can't believe you put this together for me!"

It hurts a little that he assumed I wouldn't put any effort into our relationship, but I have to remind myself that we're still getting to know each other. We spent years judging each other and seeing each other from a different perspective. All that matters is that he's giving me a chance *now* to prove him wrong.

"Of course I care about you," I say softly. I scoot closer to him, gently caressing his cheek. My heart thuds anxiously in my chest, a nervous smile blooming across my face. "I know it's only been a few days since we realized we're mates, but I'm happier than I've ever been in my life. I've enjoyed every minute we've spent together since then, and…well, I'm falling in love with you, Nico."

He lets out a sound somewhere between a laugh and a sob, giving me the biggest smile I've ever seen on his face. "I've been in love with you since I was seven years old, Quentin. And I've fallen in love with you a million times harder every day since we discovered we're mates."

This time, when he kisses me, I don't hold back. I kiss him like I'm desperate for it, pulling his clothes off as fast as possible when it feels like I'm going to explode if I don't feel his bare skin against mine. I rub my throbbing cock against his and lower him to the blankets, swallowing his gasp by covering his lips with mine again. His nails rake over my back, making me growl and buck my hips against his.

As we make out, I can practically feel the full moon beating down on us. I got a tent with mesh panels on the top so we'd be able to look up at the stars and moon tonight. When Nico wraps his legs around my waist and positions himself so my cock brushes against his tight hole, I tremble and pull away from his mouth to trail kisses along his jaw. He bares his throat to me, and I snarl as I feel my canines elongate slightly. My teeth throb with the intense need to mark him.

With trembling fingers, I reach over to grab the lube I hid under the blankets in the corner. Nico whines impatiently and grinds against me, his long cock bobbing between our stomachs. I grin and give him a quick kiss before I sit up. He might think he's ready for me to bite him and fuck him, but I want to make sure he's prepared so it'll be as good as possible for him. The second I sink my teeth into his throat, I'm gonna lose my fucking mind, along with all reason. I'll be beating myself up forever if I accidentally hurt him.

"You sure you still want this?" I ask, pouring out a generous amount of lube. I warm it up between my hands, staring down at him with admiration as my eyes flick over his lean, muscular body. Lifting his hips, I bring one of my hands down to circle his tight hole with my index finger. He squirms under me, so I finally give him what he wants and press my finger into him. He groans—the most beautiful fucking sound in the world—and I look up to meet his eyes as I slowly fuck him with my finger. "You still want me to mark you tonight, sweetheart?"

"Yes," he moans, throwing his head back to bare his throat as he arches his back. "I want that more than anything. I want you to mark me so I can mark you too."

His words spur me to move things along faster, and I insert another finger. Gotta get him nice and stretched so he can take me. Once I'm able to fit three fingers, I pull my hand away and spread some more lube over my thick cock. It's a struggle not to thrust into him too quickly—I'm still trembling as I slowly press into him inch by inch. When he starts moaning and thrusting against me, I bite my lip to keep myself from going fucking wild.

"Fuck, you feel so good." I groan, a shiver racking through my body once I'm filling him to the hilt. He wraps his legs around me to pull me closer, digging his claws into my back. I pull out of him slowly and wrap my hand around his cock, brushing my thumb over the tip where a bead of precum has accumulated. I bring my finger to my lips so I can taste him, moaning and snapping my hips against his to enter him fully again. "You were made to take my cock, weren't you? Goddess, you're the perfect mate."

He moans, mumbling incoherent nonsense as I pick up the

pace, fucking him harder and faster. As I get closer to coming, the need to mark him becomes nearly unbearable. I lean over him, using one of my hands to cup the back of his neck, and lower my mouth to his throat. He shivers violently when I scrape my teeth against him, and my wolf practically screams at me *mine, mate, mark,* over and over again.

The second my teeth sink into his skin, I come inside of him. He moans and writhes under me, and I growl as I clamp down harder and keep fucking him through my orgasm. Nobody's ever told me what it's like to mark someone, but it's so much better and more intense than anything I could have imagined. I feel closer to Nico, closer to the moon, and closer to my true nature than I ever have in my life. Goddess, I never want this moment to end.

Nico pushes me away—seconds, maybe minutes later? — and flips us so he's on top. I growl and lick my lips, greedy for the taste of his blood. I'm still inside of him and still fucking hard despite the fact that I already came.

"I wanna mark you now." Nico growls, bouncing up and down as he rides me hard. His eyes are bright and wild, his skin slick with sweat. It's not until he places his hands on my chest that I realize he came all over our stomachs. But he's still hard, just like I am. A feral grin breaks out across my face at the realization that we'll be able to keep this up all night.

"Mark me, then." I rub my hands over his muscular thighs and onto his hips, helping him fuck me even harder. "I want everyone to know I'm yours."

It's why I marked him in such an obvious spot on his throat. So that every wolf we meet will see it and know immediately he's mine.

Nico leans down to kiss and lick my chest, slowly making his way up my body. I turn my head to bare my throat, my heart racing when I feel his tongue trail from my collarbone to my neck. He chooses a visible spot like I did, sinking his teeth into my throat much more viciously than I did to him. I moan loudly and come again, his tight ass milking my cock as he continues to work on my mark. It should be painful, but it's not. The longer and deeper he bites me, the more solid our connection feels.

Our mate bond has officially snapped into place. Forever. And there's nothing anyone can do to take my mate from me. Not even my dad.

We lose track of the hours, spending the night beneath the full moon making love over and over. Just like every time we have sex, I offer to let Nico fuck me too. But tonight, he's only interested in bottoming. I'm certainly not gonna complain about that. I can only assume it's the moon influencing us, muddling our brains and bringing our base instincts to the forefront.

The sun is just starting to creep over the horizon when Nico falls asleep in my arms. My eyes are heavy and my energy is drained, but I've never been so fucking happy in my life. Staring down at him, I wonder how I got so lucky. I wonder how I could ever think I didn't want this. How could I have never wanted a mate or disliked anything about this beautiful man?

After all the shit I've been through with Felix because of my dad, every single moment with Nico as my mate is like a breath of fresh air. I can't wait to begin this new chapter of my life with him by my side, no matter where we end up.

Having Nico as my mate is going to be the best adventure I ever could have wished for.

ABOUT THE AUTHOR

Willow Hadley is a self-published author who primarily writes sugary sweet reverse harem romance. She lives on the coast of North Carolina with her husband, their dog, ferret, and two cats. She started writing in early 2018, and decided to pursue publishing in 2020. She loves character driven stories and fluffy books that give you a warm, fuzzy feeling. She's also obsessed with Disney movies, and her favorite candy is licorice.

Sign up for her newsletter here!

Cricket Kendall Series

Cricket

Wildflower

Wandering Star

Luna Witch

Charlotte Reynolds Series

Smile Like You Mean It

Everything Will Be Alright

Of Moons and Monsters Series

Of Moons and Monsters

Of Dreams and Demons